The Hopp

Written by Liz Miles
Illustrated by Rupert van Wyk

Collins

Nan has a hopper.

We hop off for food.

We zoom higher for butter.

Quick Nan! Zoom up!

We get eggs at a farm.

Look at its feet!

We get jam at a fair.

I can hear bees!

We hop on a boat for shellfish.

Hop higher!

Nan cooks eggs with leeks.

Jam tarts.
Yum!

The hopper

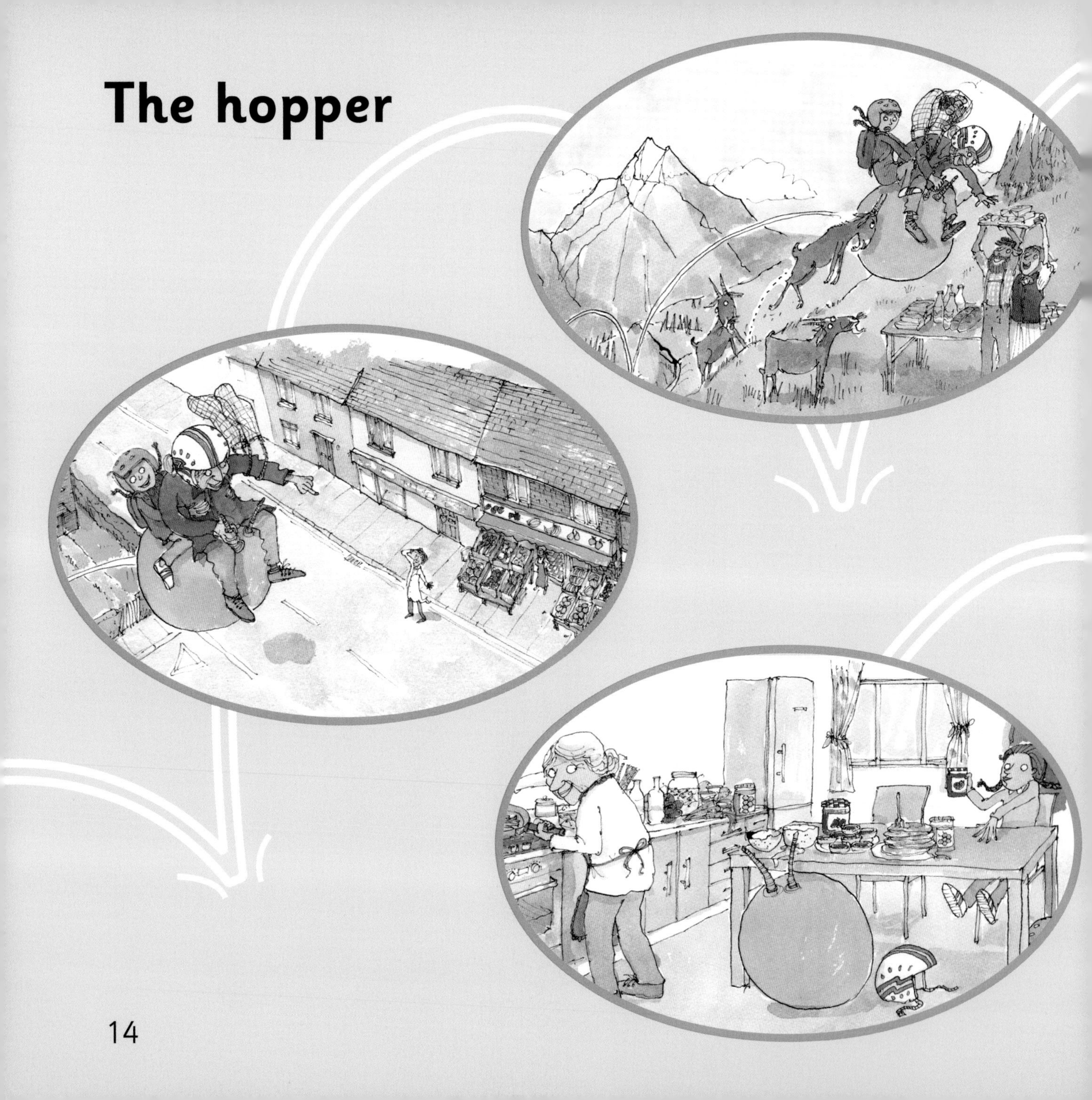

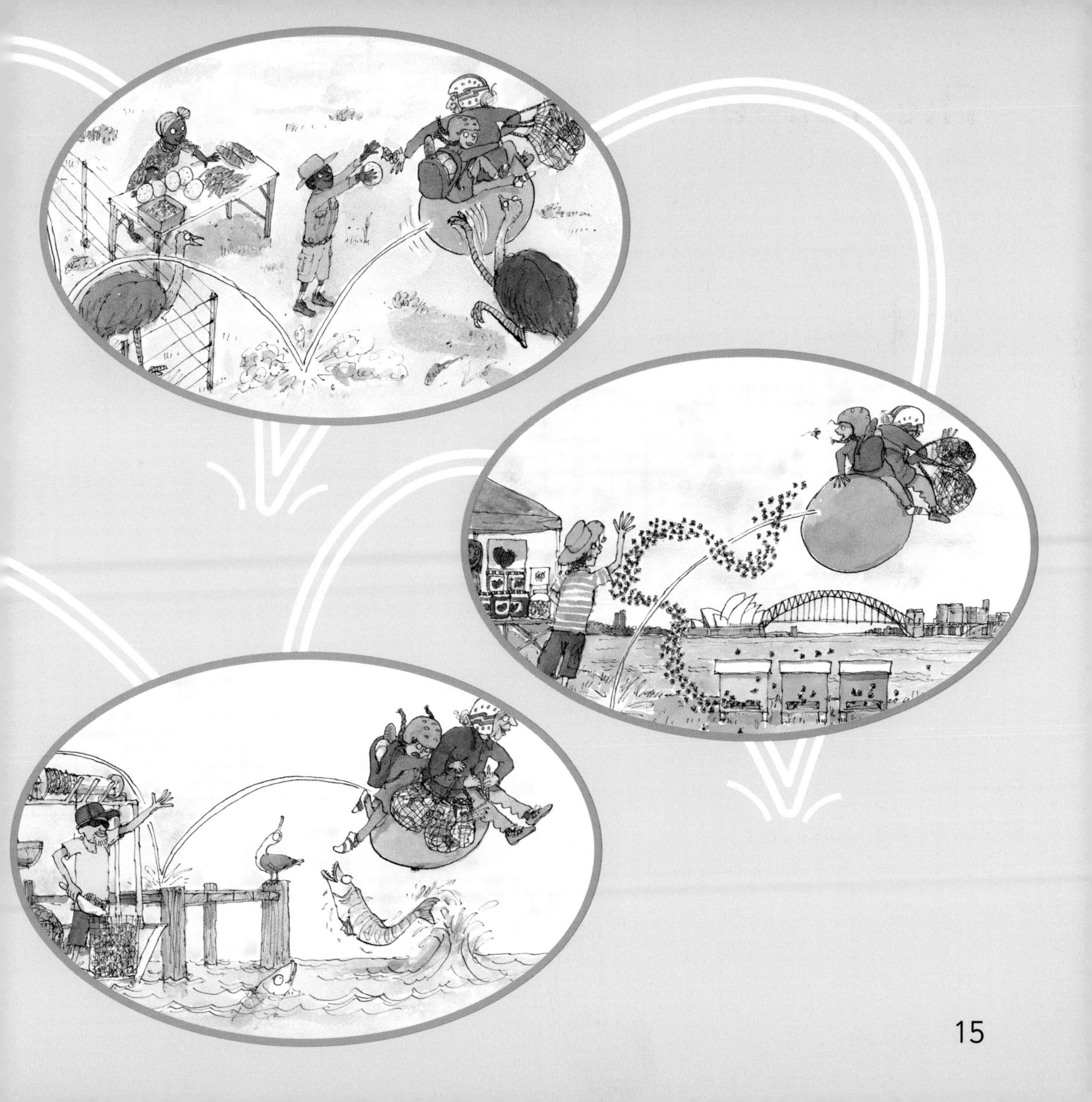

After reading

Letters and Sounds: Phase 3

Word count: 57

Focus phonemes: /ee/ /igh/ /er/ /oo/ /oo/ /ar/ /or/ /air/ /ear/ /oa/

Common exception words: I, we, the

Curriculum links: Understanding the World

Early learning goals: Reading: read and understand simple sentences, use phonic knowledge to decode regular words and read them aloud accurately

Developing fluency

- Your child may enjoy hearing you read the book.
- Look at the story map on pages 14 to 15 of the hopper's journey and ask your child to use it to help them to retell the story in their own words.

Phonic practice

- Look at the word **food** on page 3. Ask your child to segment it into its three letter sounds (phonemes) f/oo/d. Point to /oo/ and practise the sound, then ask them to sound talk and blend the sounds together.
- Do the same with the following words:

higher	h/igh/er
farm	f/ar/m
hear	h/ear
boat	b/oa/t

Extending vocabulary

- Ask your child if they can think of an antonym (opposite) for each of the following words:

higher (*lower*) off (*on*) quick (*slow*) up (*down*)